Ten Days in Hawaii

Banana Patch Press
www.bananapatchpress.com

Library of Congress Control Number: 2001127165

ISBN: 978-0-9715333-4-9

Printed in Hong Kong

Ten Days in Hawaii

by
Dr. Carolan

illustrated by
Joanna F. Carolan

Acknowledgements

Dr. Carolan would like to thank:

My wife, Joanna, for her love, support, and her beautiful illustrations.
My four sons, Sean, Seumas, Brendan, and Eamonn for the joy they have brought to my life.
All of the keikis in my practice.

Joanna F. Carolan would like to thank:

My husband, Terry, for his patience, love and sense of humor.
My family for being there when I need them.
The Banana Patch team.

They would both like to thank:

Tom Niblick of Barefoot Design Studio on Kaua'i, for his expertise and wonderful book design.
Mālia 'A. Rogers for assistance with the pronunciation of counting to ten in Hawaiian.

For Elizabeth Carolan,
who once spent ten days in Hawaii.

Aloha,

Hello!

one

On my first day in Hawaii,
what did I see?
One kitty cat dancing hula,
under a coconut tree.

two

On my second day in Hawaii,
I went to the beach.
There were two dogs surfing,
on two surfboards each!

three

On my third day in Hawaii,
I snorkeled in the sea. Three
Humuhumu-nukunuku-ā-puaʻa
were looking up at me.

four

LILIKOI   GUAVA   Y   S

On my fourth day in Hawaii,
   it was very hot.
Four geckos were eating shave ice
   (and liking it a lot)!

five

On my fifth day in Hawaii,
it rained the whole day long.
Five frogs went by in kayaks,
singing a happy song.

six

On my sixth day in Hawaii,
I saw a big rainbow.
Six dolphins jumped
over it.

Some jumped high.

Some jumped low.

seven

On my seventh day in Hawaii,
I found outside the door,
Only seven rubber slippers.

Can you help me find one more?

eight

On my eighth day in Hawaii,
 I went on a nature hike.
I saw a family with eight chicks,
 the smallest was riding a bike.

nine

9

On my ninth day in Hawaii
at a tropical fruit stand,
Nine pineapples played music
in a 'ukulele band.

ten

On my tenth day in Hawaii,
my visit was almost pau*.
By the light of ten tiki torches,
we had a big lūʻau!

* (pronounced "pow", Hawaiian word meaning done)

Let's Count
in Hawaiian

One

'Ekahi   (ay-kah´-hee)

Two

'Elua   (ay-loo´-ah)

Three

'Ekolu   (ay-koh´-loo)

Four

'Ehā   (ay-ha´)

Five

ʻElima (ay-lee´-mah)

Six
ʻEono (ay-oh´-no)

Seven
ʻEhiku (ay-hee´-koo)

Eight
ʻEwalu (ay-vah´-loo)

Nine
ʻEiwa (ay-ee´-vah)

Ten
ʻUmi (oo´-mee)

Aloha,

Good-bye!

Dr. Carolan was born in Melbourne, Australia. He moved to Hawai'i in 1977. He has been a pediatrician in private practice on the island of Kaua'i, Hawai'i since 1979. He has four sons and one granddaughter.

Joanna F. Carolan was born in San Francisco, California. Her grandparents moved to Kaua'i in 1967; she spent part of her teenage years living with them in Wailua. She is an artist and owner of Banana Patch Studio & Gallery on Kaua'i.

Other Dr. Carolan books available from Banana Patch Press:

B is for Beach, An Alphabet Book
Where Are My Slippers? A Book of Colors
Goodnight Hawaiian Moon
Old Makana Had a Taro Farm
This is My Piko
A President from Hawai'i

For more information visit:
www.bananapatchpress.com
www.bananapatchstudio.com